YOKO & FRIENDS
SCHOOL DAYS

The Secret Birthday

Text and jacket art by

Rosemary Wells

Interior illustrations by

John Nez

VOLO

Hyperion Books for Children
New York

Volo and the Volo colophon are trademarks of Disney Enterprises, Inc.

Printed in the United States of America

First Edition
1 3 5 7 9 10 8 6 4 2

LIBRARY OF CONGRESS CATALOGING-IN-PUBLICATION DATA
Wells, Rosemary.
The secret birthday / text and jacket art by Rosemary Wells; interior illustrations
by John Nez.—1st ed.
p.   cm. — (Yoko & friends—school days)
Summary: Noisy Nora finds a surprising new site for her birthday party when her mother will
not let her invite all of her classmates to her house because it is too small.
ISBN 0-7868-0729-6 (hc.) — ISBN 0-7868-1535-3 (pbk.)
[1. Birthdays—Fiction. 2. Parties—Fiction. 3. Schools—Fiction. 4. Mice—Fiction.
5. Animals—Fiction.] I. Nez, John A., ill. II. Title.
PZ7.W46843 Se 2002
[E]—dc21
2001026791

Visit www.hyperionchildrensbooks.com

On Monday morning,

Noisy Nora did not say hello

on the school bus.

She did not say anything.

3

"She looks as if she's got a whole bag of nuts in her mouth," said Timothy.

"What's in your mouth, Nora?" asked Yoko.

"Nfng," said Nora.

"Something's in your mouth,"

said Timothy.

"Scrt," said Nora.

Nora would not open her mouth.

She would not open her mouth

during the "Good Morning" song.

She did not open her mouth

during show-and-tell.

All she would say was "Bmf!"

"Something is very wrong with

Nora," said Mrs. Jenkins.

"Nora, perhaps you can tell me

about it at lunchtime."

At lunchtime, Mrs. Jenkins took

Nora to the Quiet Corner.

"What on earth is in your mouth,

Nora?" she asked.

Nora blurted it out. "A secret!"

she said.

"Oh! A secret!" said Mrs. Jenkins.

"I can't tell," said Nora.

"Well, if it is a secret, I will not ask about it," said Mrs. Jenkins.

"It's about my birthday!" said Nora.

"Your birthday?" said Mrs. Jenkins.

"Yes. My birthday party. My mama says our house is too small for a big party, so I can only have five guests."

"Oh, dear," said Mrs. Jenkins.

"Yes! And I'm not allowed to tell anyone! You said, No birthday talk at school, so I can't say anything!"

"That's the rule!" said Mrs. Jenkins.

"But I don't know who can come to the party or not!" said Nora. "Mama put the invitations in the mailbox today.

I will not know who is coming for three more days!"

"Good things are worth waiting for," said Mrs. Jenkins.

"Yes, but I don't want to wait," said Nora. "I want to find out who is coming, right now!"

"You are not allowed to do that in school, Nora," said Mrs. Jenkins. "If you do, somebody's feelings are going to be hurt."

"That's why I have to keep it in!" said Nora.

"Well, maybe you don't have to keep the secret right in your mouth," said Mrs. Jenkins.

"Yes, I do!" said Nora.

Nora kept her birthday secret right
inside her mouth for three more
days, until just before playtime.
She did not see Grace hiding in
the girls' room.

"Are you coming to my party?"

Nora whispered to Yoko.

"Yes! Who else is coming?"

whispered Yoko back.

"Timothy, Charles, Claude, and

Fritz," said Nora.

Grace waited for Yoko and Nora

to go out to the playground.

"No fair!" said Grace when she

spotted Doris by the cubbies.

"What is no fair?" asked Doris.

"We are NOT invited to Nora's

birthday party!" said Grace.

"And it's mean and no fair.

See if I invite her to my party!"

Doris thwacked her tail.

The Franks came running.

"What's up?" asked the Franks.

"Nora's having a party. We're not invited," said Doris.

Grace added, "I'm telling Mrs. Jenkins that Nora talked birthday talk in school and hurt all our feelings!"

Grace waited until everyone was

playing happily.

Then she sat down and sulked.

"What's the matter, Grace?" asked

Mrs. Jenkins.

"My feelings are hurt," said Grace.

"What happened?" asked

Mrs. Jenkins.

"Nora talked birthday talk, and we

are left out!" said Grace.

"I believe you might be talking

more birthday talk than Nora,

Grace," said Mrs. Jenkins.

"Not true! No fair!" said Grace.

On the school bus, Grace and the Franks and Doris sang "We're not invited and we don't care!" all the way home.

In her seat, Nora tried to shrink herself down to the size of a pea.

"I don't want to have any birthday party at all," said Nora to her mother.

"Why ever not?" asked Nora's mother.

"I'm running away from all of this forever," said Nora.

"Be back in time for supper," said her mother.

The next morning, Nora was the

first one on the school bus.

Henry, the bus driver, said, "Good

morning, Nora! You do not look

happy. What is the matter?"

"Everybody hates me," said Nora

in a grumpy voice.

"Everybody hates you!" said Henry.

"Why on earth would that be?"

Nora did not answer.

She glared out the window.

The school bus passed the

children's hospital.

"I would rather be in the children's hospital with two broken legs than have everybody hate me," said Nora.

"Fiddle-dee-dee!" said Henry. "I go in there all the time. I help out with the kids. Believe me, you would not want to have two broken legs and be in the hospital, Nora."

"Do they have birthdays there?"

asked Nora.

"Everybody has birthdays," said

Henry. "Even in the hospital.

They have a big cafeteria."

Nora had an idea.

After the "Good Morning" song,

she told her idea to Mrs. Jenkins.

Mrs. Jenkins asked the class for

volunteers.

"We are having a secret birthday!"

she said. "No one will know

where it is or who it is for!

Nobody will be left out!"

Saturday at lunchtime, Henry

jumped into his school bus.

The gears squeaked, and

the bus lurched onto the road.

First he picked up Nora and her

mother. They had birthday cakes.

Then he picked up Timothy.

Timothy had fifteen bags of chips.

Claude was next.

He had jelly beans.

Yoko's mother had made special sushi.

Charles brought ice cream.

Fritz had chocolate sauce.

Doris lugged squeeze cheese and

crackers.

The Franks' dad had cooked up a pot

of franks and beans.

The last stop was Grace's house.
Grace's mother helped her get
thirty sandwiches onto the bus.

"Where are we going?" asked
everybody, but Henry wouldn't
tell.

The bus stopped outside a
building where no one had ever
been before.

"Where are we?" asked Fritz.

"It's the children's hospital," said
Claude. "I can read the sign.
There is Mrs. Jenkins!"

The party was a great success.

When it was over, all the patients

in the hospital felt much better.

And so did Nora.

Dear Parents,

When our children were young we lived in a small house, but we always made a space just for books. When their dad or I would read a story out loud, the TV was always off—radio and music, too—because it intruded.

Soon this peaceful half hour of every day became like a little island vacation. Our children are lifetime readers now, with an endless curiosity for the rich world waiting between the covers of good books. It cost us nothing but time well spent and a library card.

This set of easy-to-read books is about the real nitty-gritty of elementary school. There are new friends, and bullies, too. There are germs and the "Clean Hands" song, new ways of painting pictures, learning music, telling the truth, gossiping, teasing, laughing, crying, separating from Mama, scary Halloweens, and secret valentines. The stories are all drawn from the experiences my children had in school.

It's my hope that these books will transport you and your children to a setting that's familiar, yet new, a place where you can explore the exciting new world of school together.

Rosemary Wells